I Heard You Can Draw!

A Story for Class Artists Everywhere

M. D. Savran

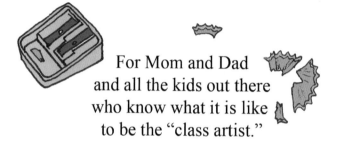

For Mom and Dad
and all the kids out there
who know what it is like
to be the "class artist."

ISBN 10: 0989649008
ISBN 13: 978-0-9896490-0-1

I Heard You Can Draw!

A Story for Class Artists Everywhere

We all have something that we *really* like to do.

It could be...

...sports,

reading,

or dance.

To name just a few.

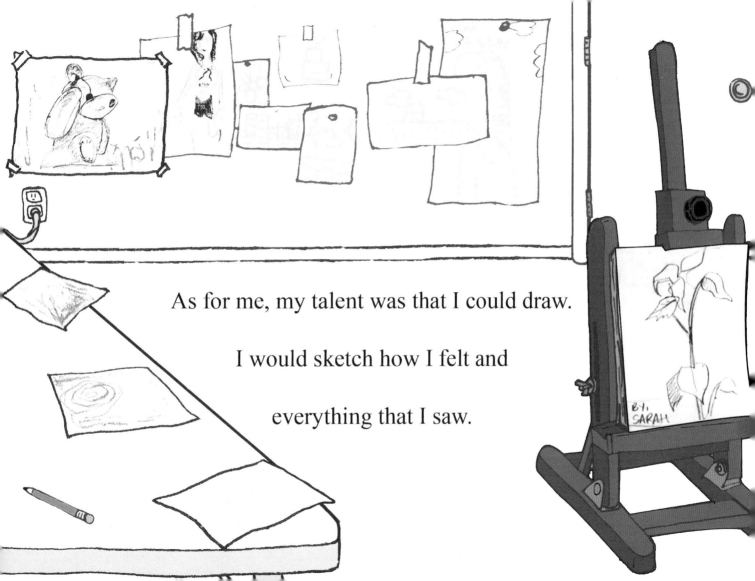

As for me, my talent was that I could draw.

I would sketch how I felt and

everything that I saw.

One day in class I could not concentrate.

I drew a picture that Mrs. Earl had to

confiscate.

She held up my drawing in front of the class

and said, "If you draw while I talk, you **_will_ _not_** pass!"

She placed my drawing face-down on her chair,

but the *whole* class had seen it and my story starts there.

After lunch a boy

came over and said,

"I heard you can draw!

Will you make me

a monster's head?"

When I gave him

the drawing,

he thought it was cool!

He showed it to *everyone* in the entire school.

Later a girl said,

"Please draw my cat!"

So I drew him.

No problem!

He was

orange and **fat**.

I kept drawing pictures for everyone I knew

and people I *didn't* know.

And even *teachers,* too!

They asked me to draw them all *kinds* of strange things.

Like spaceships in the rain and unicorns with wings!

Some wanted jets that fly really far

and a *porcupine* driving a **blue** race car!

I was drawing a princess for someone when I cried,

"Something

is wrong!

I think

my hand died!"

I went to the nurse who looked sad when I said,

"Please help me, Miss Love! My **drawing** hand is *dead!*

All she said was,

"Don't draw the things that everyone asks for.

Draw what *you* want. That's it. Nothing more."

I said, "Draw with a dead hand? How could this be?"

At home that night I couldn't smile or eat

and even worse I could **not** draw! I felt so *incomplete*.

Then I remembered what the nurse told me to do,

so with my **left** hand and a sigh I used colored pencils and drew.

I used the **red** because I felt really **mad**.

Then I used **blue** because I also felt **sad**.

When my fingers started to move

I smiled and thought,

"My **drawing** hand is better

and I *didn't* need a **shot**!"

I drew my *dog* and my *house*

and *thoughts* that I treasure.

I was drawing again!

My hand was *not* gone forever!

My hand was back and oh, I should mention

that the next day in class I paid *close* attention!

Then someone whispered, "Hey! I heard your hand is alive!

Draw me a bear attacking an angry beehive."

I **ALMOST** did but I stopped and said,

"Uh-oh,

not again!

I think my hand is dead!"

THE END.

Now it is your turn to draw whatever *you* want to draw!

This **sketchbook** belongs to:

_____

(Name)

47448504R00030

Made in the USA
Charleston, SC
11 October 2015